For the baby

Published in 1981 by The Viking Press
625 Madison Avenue, New York, New York 10022
First published in Great Britain
by Kestrel, Penguin Books Ltd,
as Peepo!

Printed in Hong Kong

2 3 4 5 6 86 85 84 83 82

Library of Congress Cataloging in Publication Data

Ahlberg, Janet.
    Peek-a-boo!
    Summary: Brief rhyming clues invite the reader to look through holes in the
pages for a baby's view of the world from breakfast to bedtime.
    1. Toy and movable books – Specimens. [1. Babies – Fiction. 2. Toy and movable
books] I. Ahlberg, Allan. II. Title.
PZ7. A2689Pe   [E]   81-1925
ISBN 0-670-54598-8   AACR2

Father

PEEK·A·BOO!

AN ALA NOTABLE BOOK

Sisters

Mother

by

Janet & Allan Ahlberg

THE VIKING PRESS, NEW YORK

Grandma

Baby in the morning

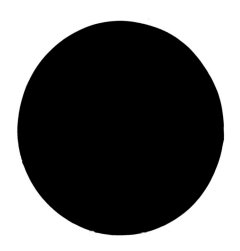

PEEK-A-BOO!

What can he see?

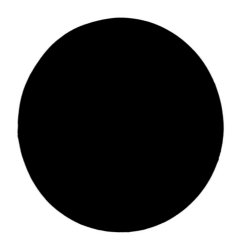

What can you?

Baby at breakfast

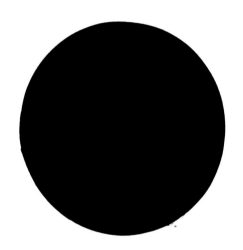

PEEK-A-BOO!

He can see his sisters

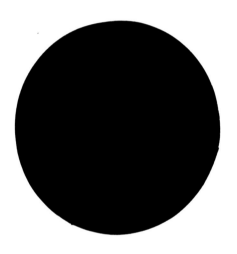

Can you?

Baby in the backyard

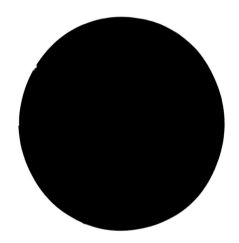

PEEK-A-BOO!

What can he see?

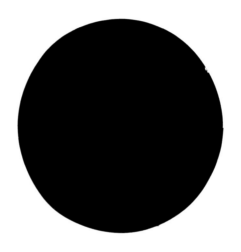

What can you?

Baby in the park

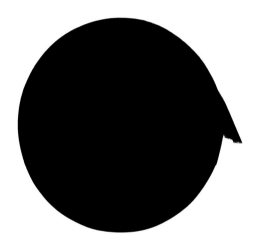

PEEK-A-BOO!

He can see three little boats

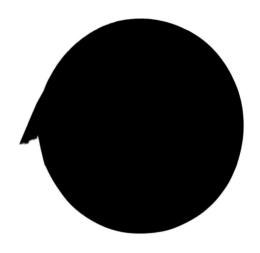

Can you?

Baby at suppertime

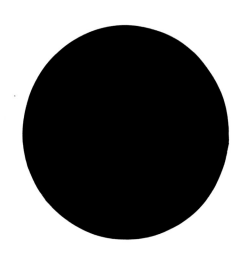

PEEK-A-BOO!

What can he see?

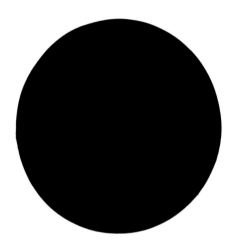

What can you?

Baby in the bath

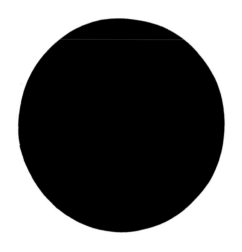

PEEK-A-BOO!

He can see a rubber duck

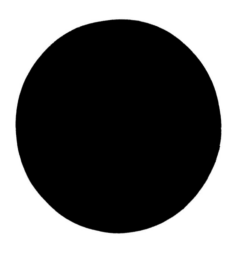

Can you?

Baby at bedtime

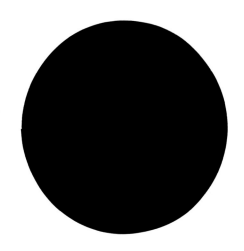

PEEK-A-BOO!

What can he see?

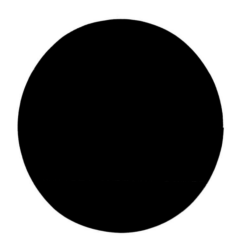

What can you?